SUPERWOMEN in STEM

Women Scientists in Astronomy and Space

NANCY DICKMANN

Gareth Stevens
PUBLISHING

Please visit our website, www.garethstevens.com.
For a free color catalog of all our high-quality books,
call toll-free 1-800-542-2595 or fax 1-877-542-2596.

Cataloging-in-Publication Data

Names: Dickmann, Nancy.
Title: Women scientists in astronomy and space / Nancy Dickmann.
Description: New York : Gareth Stevens Publishing, 2018. | Series: Superwomen in STEM | Includes index.
Identifiers: LCCN ISBN 9781538214756 (pbk.) | ISBN 9781538214039 (library bound) | ISBN 9781538214763 (6 pack)
Subjects: LCSH: Women in science--Juvenile literature. | Women astronomers--Juvenile literature. | Women scientists--Juvenile literature.
Classification: LCC Q130.D53 2018 | DDC 305.43'5--dc23

Published in 2018 by
Gareth Stevens Publishing
111 East 14th Street, Suite 349
New York, NY 10003

Copyright © 2018 Brown Bear Books Ltd

For Brown Bear Books Ltd:
Text and Editor: Nancy Dickmann
Designer and Illustrator: Supriya Sahai
Editorial Director: Lindsey Lowe
Children's Publisher: Anne O'Daly
Design Manager: Keith Davis
Picture Manager: Sophie Mortimer
Concept development: Square and Circus / Brown Bear Books Ltd

Picture Credits: Alamy: Art Collection 8, Science History Images 23, 29; istockphoto: asleelt 5, Darren Wise 14; NASA: 11, 22, 33, 39, 40, 41; Public
Domain: Astronomy Cast 35, CSIRO 34, Harvard University 26, Harvard University Library 27, Sweeper in the Sky 20, Graham Woan/University of
Glasgow 32; Science Photo Library: Harvard College Observatory 28; Shutterstock: Jejim 38, mr. Timmi 15, Yelloo 4; Thinkstock: Photos.com 16,
solarseven 10, Evgeniy Trifonov 21; Wellcome Images: 9, 17.

Character artwork © Supriya Sahai
All other artwork Brown Bear Books Ltd

Brown Bear Books has made every attempt to contact the copyright holders.
If anyone has any information please contact licensing@brownbearbooks.co.uk

Manufactured in the United States of America

CPSIA compliance information: Batch #CW18GS. For further information contact Gareth Stevens, New York, New York at 1-800-542-2595.

Contents

Looking to the Stars 4
Wang Zhenyi 6
Caroline Herschel 12
Maria Mitchell 18
Henrietta Swan Leavitt 24
Jocelyn Bell Burnell 30
Sally Ride 36

Timeline 42
Gallery 44
Science Now 45
Glossary 46
Further Information 47
Index 48

Looking to the Stars

For as long as humans have existed, people have gazed up at the stars. Over the centuries, the work of talented astronomers has helped us understand the universe.

Astronomy is the study of the universe. It began long ago, when ancient peoples began to track the movements of the sun, moon, planets, and stars. Soon, astronomers were keeping detailed records and taking a more scientific approach.

Ancient peoples used the stars to find their way — and sometimes to tell the future.

Children studying science today will be the next generation of scientists!

UNDERSTANDING THE UNIVERSE

Most early astronomers believed that Earth was at the center of the universe, and everything else revolved around it. In the 1500s, scientists began to accept that the sun was at the center, and Earth moved around it. Around the same time, the invention of the telescope let astronomers see objects in space clearly for the first time.

Now, high-tech telescopes—both on the ground and in space — expand our knowledge on a daily basis. Spacecraft have traveled to all of the planets, and even beyond the solar system. But there is still a lot to learn.

MAKING THEIR MARK

For most of history, astronomers were nearly always men. Few women went to school, and they were not expected to be interested in science. Even when women did study space, their efforts were often overlooked or ignored. That is finally changing, and many of today's top astronomers are women. But they are just the most recent in a long line of determined female scientists who broke with tradition to pursue their goals.

WANG ZHENYI

Chinese astronomer Wang Zhenyi is best known for her works on eclipses and the movement of the planets, and for her beautiful poetry.

Wang Zhenyi was born in China in 1769, at a time when women were expected to be little more than wives and mothers. She was raised by her father and her grandparents. They loved reading and learning, and they passed this love on to Zhenyi. Her grandfather taught her astronomy, and her grandmother taught her poetry. Her father taught her other subjects, such as medicine, geography, and math. The family traveled a lot within China, and Zhenyi was able to see how other people lived.

> **There were times that I had to put down my pen and sighed. But I love the subject, I do not give up.**

PUSHING BOUNDARIES

In China in the 1700s, girls were not educated like they are today. Instead, they were taught skills that would be useful once they were married, such as cooking and sewing. Girls like Zhenyi who came from wealthy, scholarly families might be taught literature and even science at home. But very few took it as far as Zhenyi was determined to do.

TEACHING HERSELF

Zhenyi's grandfather had a large library. Some sources say that he had 75 bookshelves! He owned works by Chinese scholars, as well as translations of works by European thinkers. Instead of going to school, Zhenyi learned by reading and thinking about what she had read. She was also able to discuss ideas with other scholars, including some women.

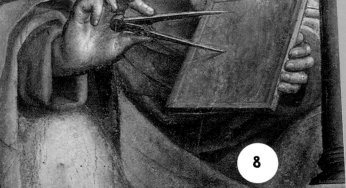

Zhenyi read the works of the Greek mathematician Euclid, translated into Chinese.

Zhenyi read everything with a critical eye. Some of her earliest writings are reviews of other scholars' work. She was very interested in math, and she wanted to make it easier for non-scholars. She wrote a simplified version of a famous Chinese math book—making both the language and the calculations easier for students to understand. She firmly believed that learning was not just for men, but was for women as well.

MARRIAGE

At the age of 25, Zhenyi married Zhan Mei, who also came from an intellectual family. He supported her learning and writing, and she continued to work throughout their marriage. She had also started writing poetry. Many of her poems were inspired by things and people she had seen on her travels. The poems showed her knowledge of history and literature.

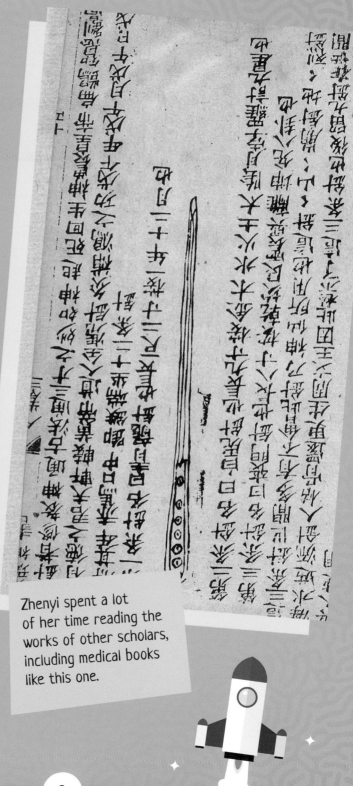

Zhenyi spent a lot of her time reading the works of other scholars, including medical books like this one.

ASTRONOMY

One of Zhenyi's greatest loves was astronomy. She made careful observations of the movement of stars and planets. Using her knowledge of mathematics, she was able to explain why they moved the way they did. She was able to correct the calculations made by earlier scholars. She also wrote down her own ideas about how the universe worked. She had her own theories about the shape of Earth and why people did not fall off of it.

DEMONSTRATING ECLIPSES

Zhenyi was interested in eclipses, both solar and lunar. A solar eclipse happens when the moon moves between Earth and the sun, appearing to block out the sun. In a lunar eclipse, Earth moves between the sun and the moon, casting a shadow that darkens the moon. Zhenyi was able to explain the causes of a lunar eclipse, which went against the accepted ideas in China at the time.

Zhenyi explained the relationship between lunar eclipses and solar eclipses like this one.

Nearly all of the physical features on Venus are named for women—including a crater named for Wang Zhenyi.

Zhenyi set up a demonstration to show how lunar eclipses happened. She put a round table in a pavilion in her garden. The table represented Earth. She hung a crystal lamp from the ceiling to represent the sun. On one side of the table, a large round mirror stood in for the moon. Zhenyi moved the three objects in relation to each other, based on what she knew of their actual movements. By watching the relationship of the lamp and the mirror, she could see how a lunar eclipse worked.

DEATH AND LEGACY

Zhenyi died in 1797 at only 29 years old. Before her death, she asked her husband to pass her writings on to her good friend, Qian Yuling. This included her poetry and her scientific writings. Qian Yuling gave them to her nephew, Qian Yiji, a famous scholar. He wrote a preface and published the works, naming Zhenyi as one of China's greatest women scholars. In 2004, a crater on the planet Venus was named in her honor.

Caroline Herschel

The astronomer William Herschel is famous for discovering Uranus. However, his sister Caroline made many of her own groundbreaking discoveries.

Caroline was born in the German city of Hanover in 1750. She was one of ten children, but three of her siblings had already died by the time Caroline was born. Her father, Isaac, played the oboe in a military band and was often away from home. Her older sister, Sophia, got married and left home when Caroline was only five, leaving Caroline as her mother's main helper around the house. At the age of 10, Caroline caught typhus, a serious disease. She survived, but it left her scarred and stunted her growth. Even as an adult, she was only 4 feet 3 inches inches (130 cm) tall.

QUICK FACTS

NAME: Caroline Herschel

BIRTH: 1750, Hanover, Germany

OCCUPATION: Musician and astronomer

EDUCATION: Self-taught

13

" It was my task to be the Cinderella of the family. "

EDUCATION

Caroline's father wanted all his children to learn mathematics, French, and music, but her brothers received more education than she did. Her mother didn't see the point of educating her. She thought that Caroline would be better off training to be a servant, since she was unlikely ever to get married. In the meantime she would have to do most of the work around the house.

MOVING ABROAD

Caroline's brother William was eleven years older than her. In 1757, he had immigrated to England to work as a musician. After their father died, he invited Caroline to go to England and join him. She would learn to sing and help to run his household. Caroline was excited about the freedom this new life would offer her. She trained as a singer and learned to play the harpsichord.

When she arrived in England, Caroline settled in the fashionable city of Bath.

Uranus was the first planet to be discovered with a telescope. The discovery led to new opportunities for William and Caroline.

Caroline also learned to speak English and took math lessons from her brother. Her music career took off, and soon she was in demand as a soloist.

A NEW PASSION

However, William was becoming less interested in music. His new passion was astronomy. He began to spend more and more time on it. Caroline supported him in this new direction, even though it meant abandoning her singing career. She found astronomy fascinating, and she spent long hours copying out his astronomy catalogs and papers.

William was frustrated with the quality of telescopes available, so he began to make his own. Caroline learned how to grind lenses for the telescopes, and made notes of her brother's observations. In 1781, William made his big discovery—the planet Uranus. As a reward, he was named "The King's Astronomer."

❝ I found I was to be trained for an assistant astronomer, and by way of encouragement a telescope adapted for 'sweeping' was given me. ❞

SWEEPING THE SKY

Caroline began to make her own discoveries. She used a methodical process of "sweeping the sky," moving her telescope to observe vertical strips of sky, looking for interesting objects. In 1783 she discovered a new nebula. William built her a new telescope, which she used to search for comets. She discovered her first in 1786.

In addition to her own scientific work, Caroline continued to act as William's secretary and housekeeper. He stood at his telescope and called out his observations to Caroline, who wrote them down. In 1787, the king of England granted her an annual salary of £50 for her work as William's assistant, making her the first woman to be paid for her work in astronomy.

NEW DISCOVERIES

As the years passed, Caroline came out from her brother's shadow and began to be recognized as an astronomer in her own right.

Caroline did much of her work for King George III of England.

She discovered eight comets and fourteen nebulae. She also checked and corrected an existing star catalog, adding hundreds of stars that had not been included in the original version.

DEATH AND LEGACY

In 1828, the Royal Astronomical Society awarded Caroline a gold medal for her work on a huge catalog of over 2,500 nebulae. It would be more than 150 years before another woman received the same award. In her nineties, she was awarded the gold medal of science by the king of Prussia.

Caroline died at the age of 97 in 1848. Several of the comets she discovered are named for her, along with an asteroid and a crater on the moon.

Caroline's patience and curious mind led her to make many new discoveries.

Maria Mitchell

Maria Mitchell was a teacher and librarian. But she was also more than that — she was a talented astronomer and a pioneer of women's rights.

Maria was born in 1818 on the Massachusetts island of Nantucket, a center of the whaling industry. Her family belonged to a religious group called Quakers. Unlike many other people at that time, the Quakers believed that girls had just as much right to an education as boys. With many of the men often away on long whaling voyages, Nantucket women had a reputation for being capable and independent. It was the perfect start for a girl who loved learning.

> **66 We especially need imagination in science. It is not all mathematics, nor all logic, but it is somewhat beauty and poetry. 99**

DISCOVERING ASTRONOMY

Maria's father was interested in science and astronomy, and he shared this love with his daughter. He made astronomical observations to help the whalers with their navigation. Maria often helped him with the calculations. In 1831, she observed a solar eclipse with him.

TEACHER AND LIBRARIAN

At the age of just 16, Maria became a teaching assistant at her former school. The next year, she started her own school. However, just a year later she left that job to become the first librarian at the Atheneum, a private library in Nantucket. The job left her with plenty of time to read and learn about subjects that interested her—and she kept watching the skies with her telescope as well.

In her spare time, Maria read books on math and astronomy, and scanned the skies.

Comets are lumps of ice and rock that streak across the sky as they travel in long, looping orbits around the sun.

"MISS MITCHELL'S COMET"

On the night of October 1, 1847, Maria had her telescope set up on the roof of the Pacific National Bank, where her father worked. She spotted an unusual object. It was a new comet that had never been seen by anyone before. Maria reported her discovery, which soon became known as "Miss Mitchell's Comet." It made her famous, and the following year she became the first woman ever to be elected to the American Academy of Arts and Sciences.

PROFESSOR MITCHELL

The discovery of her comet opened doors for Maria. In the late 1850s, she traveled in the United States and Europe, seeing the sights and meeting fellow scientists. In 1865 she became the first professor hired to teach at Vassar College, a new college founded to educate women. She lived in the college's observatory, where she and her students observed sunspots and a transit of Venus across the sun. She was a popular professor who sometimes took her students on long trips to observe solar eclipses.

WOMEN'S RIGHTS

In 1870, Maria and another woman who was a Vassar professor discovered that they were being paid significantly less than some of the male professors—even some who were younger and less experienced. The two women complained to the college administration. They had to fight, but they finally got

During her time in England, Maria met Sir George Airy, the Astronomer Royal, and Sir John Herschel, who was the nephew of Caroline Herschel.

Transits of Venus are rare events in which the planet Venus can be seen as a dark dot as it moves across the sun.

equal pay. Maria had always thought that women—including herself—could be the intellectual equals of men. She began to take more of an interest in women's rights. In 1873 she helped to found the Association for the Advancement of Women.

HONORS

Today, Maria is recognized as an inspiring teacher and a groundbreaking astronomer. In addition to her famous comet, she has had a ship, a train, and a moon crater named after her! After her death in 1889, at the age of 70, some of her friends, family, and former students set up the Maria Mitchell Association. It honors her achievements, preserves her work, and teaches about science.

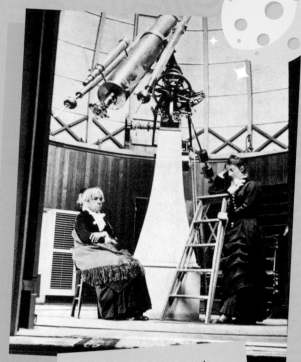

Maria (seated) trained Mary Whitney, who took over as head of Vassar's astronomy department when Maria retired.

GOLD MEDAL

King Frederick VI of Denmark was an amateur astronomer. He offered a gold medal to anyone who discovered a new comet. Although he died in 1839, the next king of Denmark, Christian VIII, continued the tradition. Maria received one of these medals in 1848.

Henrietta Swan Leavitt

About 100 years ago, a researcher published a paper about stars that change in brightness. Her breakthrough would change astronomy forever.

Henrietta Swan Leavitt was born in 1868 in Lancaster, Massachusetts. She was the oldest of seven children. Two of her siblings died as babies, and Henrietta herself was often sick—illness plagued her for the rest of her life. Her father was a church minister, and his work meant that the family often moved to different places around the country. They lived for several years in Cleveland, Ohio, and Henrietta enrolled at the nearby Oberlin college in 1886.

QUICK FACTS

NAME: Henrietta Swan Leavitt

BIRTH: 1868, Lancaster, Massachusetts

OCCUPATION: Astronomer

EDUCATION: Radcliffe College

COLLEGE LIFE

After a couple of years at Oberlin, Henrietta"s family moved to Cambridge, Massachusetts, where Harvard University is located. Harvard only accepted male students at that time, so Henrietta took classes at its sister school for women (later called Radcliffe College). During her last year, she took a class in astronomy and discovered that she loved it. After graduating in 1892, she volunteered as a research assistant at Harvard's observatory.

CATALOGING STARS

Henrietta's job at the observatory was recording the brightness of stars. The brightness of some of these stars varied over time. The stars would start off dim, then gradually—over seconds to years—they would grow brighter and then dim again. Henrietta's job was to compare photographs of the night sky taken at different times, looking for tiny differences. It was tedious work, but it suited Henrietta's precise, meticulous nature.

Radcliffe College (pictured here) merged with Harvard in 1999.

The careful, methodical work of the women "computers" led to many new discoveries.

HUMAN COMPUTER

Henrietta left the observatory in 1896 to travel in Europe. She then joined her family in their new home in Wisconsin. During this time, an illness severely damaged her hearing. In 1902, she was offered a full-time job back at the Harvard observatory. She became one of dozens of women employed as "computers." There were no electronic computers back then, so these women did all the calculations and analysis that is now left to machines.

PAY RAISE

Edward Pickering was the director of Harvard's observatory, and he valued Henrietta's work. He wrote her a letter, saying, "I should be willing to pay thirty cents an hour in view of the quality of your work, although our usual price, in such cases, is twenty-five cents an hour."

> " A straight line can readily be drawn among each of the two series of points corresponding to maxima and minima, thus showing that there is a simple relation between the brightness of the variables and their periods. "

IMPORTANT BREAKTHROUGH

Back at Harvard, Henrietta continued her previous work of analyzing variable stars. She found and cataloged 1,777 variable stars in the same section of the sky. These became known as Cepheid variable stars. Henrietta noticed that the brighter stars seemed to change brightness on a longer cycle. In 1912 she published data that proved the brightness of a star was related to the speed of its pulsing.

This was a huge breakthrough. At that time, astronomers had no clear idea of how big the universe was, or how far away many stars were. In fact, no one yet knew that the universe extended beyond our own galaxy.

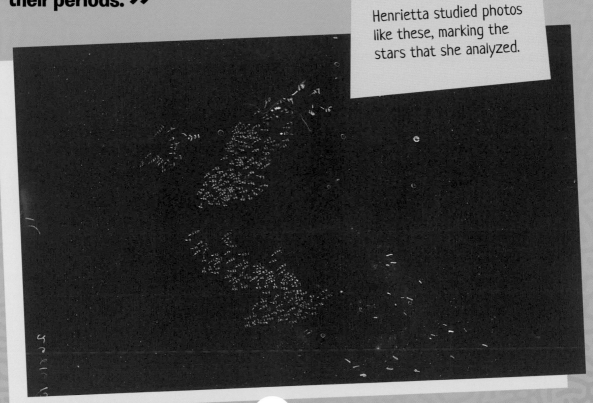

Henrietta studied photos like these, marking the stars that she analyzed.

BEYOND THE MILKY WAY

Henrietta's discovery meant that astronomers could calculate how bright these stars actually were, not just how bright they appeared from Earth. Astronomers could then calculate the stars' distance from Earth. Several years later, Edwin Hubble used a Cepheid variable star in the Andromeda Nebula to calculate its distance. He proved that Andromeda was a separate galaxy, far beyond our own galaxy, the Milky Way.

DENIED RECOGNITION

Henrietta was appointed head of the department of stellar photometry at Harvard in 1921, but she died from stomach cancer later that year, at the age of just 53. Sadly, she received little recognition for her discoveries. Other astronomers took much of the credit.

Several years after Henrietta's death, a Swedish academic tried to nominate her for the Nobel Prize in Physics, only to discover that she had already died. The prize can only be awarded to living scientists.

Although she received little recognition during her life, Henrietta was honored with an asteroid and a crater on the moon named for her.

Jocelyn Bell Burnell

Henrietta Swan Leavitt had studied the brightness of stars. Jocelyn Bell Burnell discovered a whole new type of star called a pulsar.

Jocelyn was born in 1943 in Northern Ireland, part of the United Kingdom. Her father was an architect, and one of his projects was designing a nearby planetarium, a building where images of stars, planets, and constellations are projected on the ceiling. Jocelyn was inspired by this and loved reading about astronomy. However, girls were not allowed to study science at her school. Her parents protested, and Jocelyn was allowed to join the boys' science class. At the end of the term, she got the highest grade.

QUICK FACTS

NAME: Jocelyn Bell Burnell

BIRTH: 1943, Belfast, Northern Ireland

OCCUPATION: Astronomer

EDUCATION: University of Glasgow, University of Cambridge

> 66 I switched on the high speed recorder and it came blip.... blip.... blip.... blip.... blip.... It has to be some new kind of star, not seen before. 99

EDUCATION

Despite her science grades, Jocelyn failed the exam that would allow her to go to a top local school. Her family decided to send her to a boarding school in England. She did well, and when she finished, she went on to the University of Glasgow, in Scotland, where she earned a degree in physics. After that, she began work on a PhD in astrophysics at the University of Cambridge, in England.

Computers were still just beginning to be designed. Jocelyn's telescope produced its data on a strip of paper—about 96 feet (29 m) of it every day! She spent hours reading the data, inch by inch, looking for signals from distant objects called quasars.

It may not look much like a telescope, but this array can pick up radio signals from deep space.

"LITTLE GREEN MAN"

One day Jocelyn found marks showing a series of regularly spaced pulses. They were too fast and regular to have come from a quasar. Jocelyn thought at first that they might just be interference from something much closer to Earth.

Working with her supervisor, Anthony Hewish, she began to rule out possible sources. As a joke, they named the unknown source "LGM-1," which was short for "Little Green Man."

Astronomers think quasars are linked to black holes. When matter gets absorbed into the black hole, energy is released.

RADIO TELESCOPES

Jocelyn's research at Cambridge focused on the use of radio telescopes. You don't look into a radio telescope to see the sky. Instead, it picks up the radio waves that are emitted by objects in space. During her first two years at Cambridge, Jocelyn helped to build a large radio telescope, hammering poles into a muddy field and stringing cables between them. The finished telescope covered an area the size of 57 tennis courts.

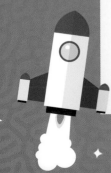

66 Women view the conventional wisdom from a slightly different angle — and that sometimes means they can clearly point to flaws in the logic, gaps in the argument, they can give a different perspective of what science is. **99**

PULSARS

It became clear that Jocelyn had discovered an entirely new kind of object. Using more sensitive equipment, she and Hewish found more signals of the same type, but coming from different parts of space. They eventually realized that the signals must be coming from neutron stars. These super-dense objects are formed when a massive star "dies" in a giant explosion called a supernova. The explosion leaves behind a small, dense core that spins rapidly. As it spins, it releases regular pulses of radio waves. These objects were named "pulsars" because of the way they pulsed.

This radio telescope in Australia has found more than half of all the pulsars that are known today.

NOBEL SNUB

Hewish was the first author listed on the academic paper that announced their discovery to the world. Jocelyn was second, followed by three others. However, when Hewish was awarded the 1974 Nobel Prize for the discovery, he shared it with another astronomer, Martin Ryle. As a research student, Jocelyn was left out, even though she had discovered the first signal.

FURTHER WORK

Jocelyn worked part-time for many years while she raised her son. She studied all types of energy coming from space, from radio waves to gamma rays and x-rays. She has also helped teach the next generation of astronomers and has received many honors, including serving as the president of the UK's Royal Astronomical Society.

In 2007, Jocelyn was made a Dame (the female equivalent of a knighthood in the UK) for her contributions to astronomy.

Neutron stars are so dense that a single teaspoon of their matter would weigh about 1 billion tons!

Sally Ride

Sally Ride wasn't content to look at the stars —
she wanted to be up among them! She became
the United States' first woman astronaut.

Sally was born in Encino, a neighborhood of Los Angeles, in 1951. Her father was a college professor and her mother volunteered at a women's prison. They encouraged Sally and her younger sister to be curious about exploring the world. Sally was good at sports, especially tennis. She thought about becoming a professional tennis player, but her love of science made her choose college instead.

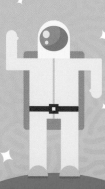

QUICK FACTS

NAME: Sally Kristen Ride

BIRTH: 1951, Los Angeles, California

OCCUPATION: Physicist and astronaut

EDUCATION: Stanford University

> 66 **Young girls need to see role models in whatever careers they may choose, just so they can picture themselves doing those jobs someday. You can't be what you can't see. 99**

COLLEGE

Sally took classes at two other colleges before enrolling at Stanford University as a junior. She graduated in 1973 with a double degree in English and physics. She then stayed at Stanford to complete a master's degree in physics, followed by a PhD in the same subject. Her research was mainly on X-rays and how they interacted with the interstellar medium (the matter that fills the space between solar systems in a galaxy).

ASTRONAUT SELECTION

While she was at Stanford, Sally saw an advertisement in the student newspaper, looking for people to apply to NASA's astronaut training program. She was one of 8,000 people who applied. Only 35 people were chosen, and only 6 were women. One of them was Sally.

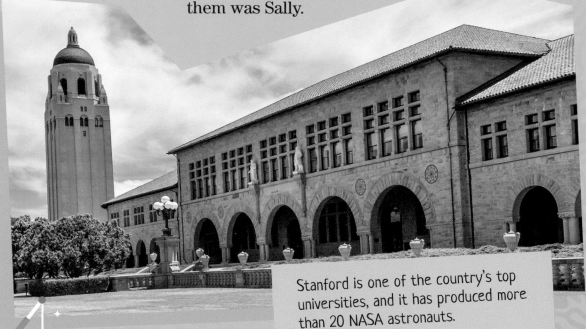

Stanford is one of the country's top universities, and it has produced more than 20 NASA astronauts.

Mission commander Robert Crippen (center) chose Sally for the space shuttle flight because of her expertise using the robot arm.

She began the intensive training program in 1978 and qualified as a mission specialist the following year. While waiting to be assigned to a space mission, she worked as ground support for other missions and helped to develop the space shuttle's robot arm.

FIRST MISSION

Sally's first mission into space began when the space shuttle *Challenger* launched on June 18, 1983. Her expertise with the shuttle's robot arm was put to the test. With her colleagues, Sally successfully used it to launch and retrieve satellites from orbit. The mission lasted 6 days, and during that time *Challenger* orbited the Earth 97 times.

Becoming America's first woman astronaut got Sally a lot of attention. At one press conference, a reporter asked her if she cried when things went wrong on the job. Sally replied, "How come nobody ever asks Rick [the shuttle's pilot] those questions?"

> **I would like to be remembered as someone who was not afraid to do what she wanted to do, and as someone who took risks along the way in order to achieve her goals.**

LATER MISSIONS

Sally's second mission into space was on *Challenger* again, in 1984. One of Sally's crewmates, Kathryn Sullivan, became the first woman to perform a spacewalk. Sally was in charge of the robotic arm again, using it to readjust a radar antenna and clear ice from the outside of the shuttle. Sally was training for her third mission when *Challenger* exploded on launch in 1986, killing its crew. This put a temporary halt to the shuttle program.

After the *Challenger* disaster, the shuttle fleet was grounded for almost three years while NASA introduced new safety measures.

WORK AFTER SPACE

President Reagan set up a commission to investigate the causes of the *Challenger* disaster, and Sally was a member. She left NASA in 1987 and became a physics professor at the University of California in San Diego. She later served as director of the California Space Institute. In 2003, she returned to NASA to help investigate the accident that destroyed the space shuttle *Columbia*.

INSPIRING OTHERS

Sally wanted to inspire others to follow their dreams. In 2001, she cofounded a company called Sally Ride Science, with the aim of encouraging girls to develop a passion for science. The organization is now a charity providing teacher training and science workshops for students. Sally also wrote seven science books for children. Her own passion for science and inspiring others led her to be inducted into the National Women's Hall of Fame and the Astronaut Hall of Fame. In 2013, she was posthumously awarded the Presidential Medal of Freedom, which is the country's highest civilian honor.

Sally Ride died in 2012, at the age of just 61, but her story continues to inspire young scientists.

Timeline

1610	Galileo uses a newly-invented telescope to discover the moons of Jupiter.
1750	Caroline Herschel is born in Germany.
1769	Wang Zhenyi is born in China.
1781	William Herschel discovers the planet Uranus.
1784	Charles Messier publishes a catalog of star clusters and nebulae that is still used today.
1786	Caroline Herschel discovers her first comet.
1797	Wang Zhenyi dies.
1801	Giuseppe Piazzi discovers the first asteroid.
1818	Maria Mitchell is born in Massachusetts.
1846	Using mathematical calculations by Urbain Le Verrier, Johann Gottfried Galle discovers the planet Neptune.
1847	Maria Mitchell discovers her first comet.
1848	Caroline Herschel dies.
1865	Maria Mitchell becomes a professor of astronomy at Vassar College.
1868	Henrietta Swan Leavitt is born in Massachusetts.
1889	Maria Mitchell dies.
1912	Henrietta Swan Leavitt publishes breakthrough data on the brightness of variable stars.
1921	Henrietta Swan Leavitt dies.

1924	Using Leavitt's discovery, Edwin Hubble proves that the universe extends beyond the Milky Way.
1930	Clyde Tombaugh discovers the planet Pluto (now considered a dwarf planet).
1943	Jocelyn Bell is born in Northern Ireland.
1951	Sally Ride is born in California.
1957	The first satellite, Sputnik, is launched into space.
1961	Russian astronaut Yuri Gagarin becomes the first person to orbit the Earth.
1963	Russian astronaut Valentina Tereshkova becomes the first woman in space.
1967	Jocelyn Bell Burnell picks up the first radio signal from a pulsar.
1969	Astronauts land on the moon for the first time.
1974	Anthony Hewish and Martin Ryle are awarded the Nobel Prize in Physics for their work on pulsars, but Jocelyn Bell Burnell is ignored.
1983	Sally Ride becomes the first American woman to travel into space.
1984	Sally Ride goes on her second mission into space.
1986	The space shuttle *Challenger* explodes during takeoff, killing all seven crew members.
1998	Construction begins on the International Space Station.
2003	The space shuttle *Columbia* disintegrates while re-entering Earth's atmosphere, killing all seven crew members.
2012	Sally Ride dies.
2013	Sally Ride is awarded the Presidential Medal of Freedom.

Gallery

The scientists covered in this book are only a few of the women who have advanced the study of space sciences, but here are more who achieved great things.

Hypatia of Alexandria (c. 370-415)

A Greek mathematician and astronomer who lived in Alexandria, Egypt. She continued the work of her father, another astronomer, and worked to preserve the knowledge of Greek astronomers who had gone before. She was murdered during a period of religious unrest in Alexandria.

Maria Margarethe Kirch (1670-1720)

A German astronomer who became the first woman to discover a comet. In 1692, she married Gottfried Kirch, another astronomer, and they worked together, producing calendars that included phases of the moon, positions of the planets, and times of sunrise and sunset. In 1702, Maria discovered a comet.

Annie Jump Cannon (1863-1941)

Another of the "human computers" who worked at the Harvard College Observatory at the same time as Henrietta Swan Leavitt. Cannon focused on recording, classifying, and cataloging tens of thousands of stars. She developed a new system of classification for stars, which is still used today.

Cecilia Payne-Caposchkin (1900-1979)

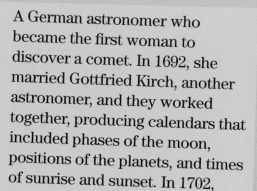

An England-born astronomer who moved to the United States after studying at Cambridge University. While researching her PhD thesis, she made the discovery that stars are made mainly of hydrogen and helium. She later became a professor at Harvard University.

Katherine Johnson (born 1918)

An American physicist and mathematician who worked at NASA. She is an expert at using computers to plan the launch windows and trajectories for spacecraft. As an African American woman, she faced many challenges in pursing her career. Her story was told in the 2016 film *Hidden Figures*.

Vera Rubin (1928-2016)

An American astronomer who studied the speed of stars. Her observations provided evidence for the existence of dark matter (a mysterious substance that cannot be detected because it gives off no energy). She was an advocate of women in science.

Carolyn Shoemaker (born 1929)

An American astronomer who searches for comets. In 1993, she and her husband discovered fragments of a broken comet orbiting Jupiter. The following year, astronomers watched as the comet crashed into Jupiter's surface.

SCIENCE NOW

We have come a long way from the days when astronomers had only basic telescopes to search the sky, or when "human computers" made difficult computations to classify stars. Astronomers today are studying the furthest reaches of the universe.

There are still many mysteries to solve. Today, cutting-edge tools are searching for exoplanets, which are planets in other solar systems. We are looking for the truth about the mysterious substance called dark matter. Could the next big discovery be yours?

It's easy to get involved in astronomy! Local astronomy clubs are great places to learn how to use a telescope. Keep up to date with the latest astronomical discoveries. Maybe someday you will make your own!

Glossary

astronomer Scientist who studies space and the objects in it.

black hole Object in space with gravity so strong that nothing can escape it.

comet Icy object that travels around the sun, forming a long, bright tail as it melts.

crater Hollow area formed when one object in space crashes into another.

eclipse The temporary blocking from view of the sun, moon, or other object.

energy The ability to do work. Energy can exist in many forms, including visible light, radio waves, and X-rays.

galaxy Group of billions of stars and other objects, held together by gravity.

harpsichord Musical instrument similar to a piano.

matter Anything that has mass and takes up space.

Milky Way The galaxy in which our solar system is located.

navigation Finding your way by using compass, stars, or other method.

nebula Cloud of gas and dust in space.

neutron star A type of extremely dense star.

Nobel Prize Prestigious prize awarded each year for achievements in different areas, including physics and chemistry.

observatory Building designed for studying space.

orbit One complete trip around Earth (or another body) in space.

physics The science of matter and energy, and of their relationship.

pulsar Object in space that emits short, repeating pulses of radio waves.

Quaker Member of a particular Christian religious group.

quasar Type of distant object in space that sends out powerful radio waves.

radio telescope Type of telescope designed to pick up radio waves.

solar system The planets, moons, and other objects that orbit a star.

space shuttle Reusable spacecraft that carried astronauts into space and back.

spacewalk An astronaut moving around outside a spacecraft in space.

stellar photometry Branch of astronomy that deals with the accurate measurement of the brightness of stars.

supernova Very bright object that results from the explosion of a star.

transit When one object in space travels across the face of a larger object.

variable star Star that appears to change in brightness over time.

Further Information

Books

Aguilar, David A. *Space Encyclopedia: A Tour of our Solar System and Beyond.* National Geographic Children's Books, 2013.

Ignotofsky, Rachel. *Women in Science: 50 Fearless Pioneers Who Changed the World.* Ten Speed Press, 2016.

Lippincott, Kristen. *Astronomy (DK Eyewitness Books).* Dorling Kindersley, 2013.

Noyce, Pendred. *Magnificent Minds: 16 Pioneering Women in Science and Medicine.* Tumblehome Learning, 2016.

Owen, Ruth. *Astronomers (Out of the Lab: Extreme Jobs in Science).* Powerkids Press, 2013.

Websites

Check out NASA's stellar website for more space info!

https://solarsystem.nasa.gov/kids/index.cfm

Learn more about space at this interactive site.

http://www.astronomy.com/

Read real-life astronomer's answers to questions about space.

coolcosmos.ipac.caltech.edu/asks

Find out how to start your own STEM career here!

http://www.stemcenterusa.com/

Index

A
Airy, Sir George 22
American Academy of Arts
    and Sciences 21
Andromeda 29
Association for the
    Advancement of
    Women 23
asteroids 17, 29
astronauts 36–41

B
black holes 33
Burnell, Jocelyn Bell 30–35

C
California Space Institute 41
Cannon, Annie Jump 44
careers in science 45
Cepheid variable stars 28, 29
Challenger space shuttle 39,
    40, 41
comets 16, 17, 21, 44, 45
craters 11, 17, 23, 29

D E
dark matter 45
eclipses 10–11, 20, 22
education 8, 14, 18, 24, 26,
    30, 32, 38

F G
Frederick VI of Denmark 23
galaxies 29, 38
gamma rays 35

H
Herschel, Caroline 12–17
Herschel, Sir John 22
Herschel, William 12, 14

Hewish, Anthony 33, 34, 35
Hubble, Edwin 29
"human computers" 27, 44
Hypatia of Alexandria 44

I J
interstellar medium 38
Johnson, Katherine 45

K L
Kirch, Maria Margarethe 44
Leavitt, Henrietta Swan
    24–29
lunar eclipses 10–11

M
medals 17, 23, 41
Mitchell, Maria 18–23

N
National Women's Hall
    of Fame 41
nebulae 16, 17
neutron stars 34, 35
Nobel Prize 29, 35

P
pay 22, 27
Payne-Caposchkin, Cecilia
    44
planetariums 30
professorships 22, 41
pulsars 34

Q
Qian Yiji 11
Quakers 18
quasars 32, 33

R
radio telescopes 32, 33, 34
radio waves 34, 35
Ride, Sally 36–41
role models 38
Royal Astronomical Society
    17, 35
Rubin, Vera 45

S
Shoemaker, Carolyn 45
solar eclipses 10, 20, 22
space shuttles 39, 40
spacewalks 40
star catalogs 17
star classification 44
stars, brightness of 26, 28,
    29
Sullivan, Kathryn 40
supernovae 34

T
telescopes 5, 15, 16, 32, 33,
    34
Tereshkova, Valentina 43
transits of Venus 22

U V
Uranus 12, 15
Venus 11, 22

W X
Wang Zhenyi 6–11
Whitney, Mary 23
women's rights 23
X-rays 35, 38